Old Turtle

Text by Douglas Wood
Watercolors by Cheng-Khee Chee

 Pfeifer-Hamilton Publishers

Pfeifer-Hamilton Publishers
210 West Michigan Duluth MN 55802-1908
218-727-0500

Pfeifer-Hamilton Publishers
210 West Michigan
Duluth MN 55802-1908 218-727-0500

Old Turtle

Printed in the Republic of Korea
by Dong-A Publishing and Printing Company, Ltd

20

Editorial Director, Susan Gustafson
Art Director, Joy Morgan Dey
Design Consultant, Patricia Boman
Production Coordinator, Tina P Olson
Library of Congress Catalog Card Number: 91-73527

ISBN 0-938586-48-3

Once, long long ago . . .
yet somehow, not so very long . . .

when all the animals

and rocks

and winds and waters

and trees

and birds

and fish

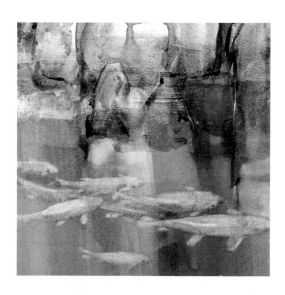

and all the beings of the world
could speak . . .
and understand one another . . .

There began . . . AN ARGUMENT.

It began softly at first . . .

Quiet as the first breeze that whispered,
"He is a wind who is never still."

Quiet as the stone that answered,
"He is a great rock that never moves."

Gentle as the mountain that rumbled,
"God is a snowy peak, high above the clouds."

And the fish in the ocean that answered, "God is a swimmer, in the dark blue depths of the sea."

"No," said the star,
    "God is a twinkling
    and a shining,
    far, far away."

"No," replied the ant,
    "God is a sound
    and a smell and a feeling,
    who is very, very close."

"God," insisted the antelope,
    "is a runner, swift and free,
    who loves to leap
    and race with the wind."

"She is a great tree,"
    murmured the willow,
    "a part of the world,
    always growing
    and always giving."

"You are wrong,"
    argued the island,
    "God is separate and apart."

"God is like the shining sun,
    far above all things,"
    added the blue sky.

"No, He is a river,
    who flows through the very
    heart of things,"
    thundered the waterfall.

"She is a hunter," roared the lion.
"God is gentle," chirped the robin.
"He is powerful," growled the bear.

And the argument

grew LOUDER

and LOUDER

and LOUDER...

until . . .

STOP!

A new voice spoke.

It rumbled loudly, like thunder.
    And it whispered softly, like butterfly sneezes.

The voice seemed to come from . . .
    why it seemed to come from . . .

. . . Old Turtle!

Old Turtle hardly ever said anything,
    and certainly never argued about God.

But now Old Turtle began to speak.

"God is indeed deep,"
    she said to the fish in the sea;
    "and much higher than high,"
    she told the mountains.

"He is swift and free as the wind,
    and still and solid as a great rock,"
    she said to the breezes and stones.

"She is the life of the world,"
    Turtle said to the willow.
    "Always close by, yet beyond
    the farthest twinkling light,"
    she told the ant and the star.

"God is gentle and powerful.
    Above all things
    and within all things.

"God is all that we dream of,
    and all that we seek,"
    said Old Turtle,
    "all that we come from
    and all that we can find.

"God IS."

Old Turtle had never said so much before.
All the beings of the world were surprised,
and became very quiet.

But Old Turtle had one more thing to say.

"There will soon be
a new family of beings in the world," she said,
"and they will be strange and wonderful.

"They will be reminders of all that God is.

"They will come in many colors and shapes,
    with different faces
    and different ways of speaking.

"Their thoughts will soar to the stars,
    but their feet will walk the earth.

"They will possess many powers.
They will be strong, yet tender,
    a message of love from God to the earth,
    and a prayer from the earth back to God."

And the people came.

But the people forgot.
They forgot that they were
    a message of love,
    and a prayer from the earth.

And they began to argue . . .
    about who knew God,
    and who did not;
    and where God was,
    and was not;
    and whether God was,
    or was not.

And often the people
    misused their powers,
    and hurt one another.
    Or killed one another.

And they hurt the earth.

Until finally even the forests
    began to die . . .

. . . and the rivers
and the oceans
and the plants and the animals
and the earth itself . . .

Because the people could not
remember who they were,
or where God was.

Until one day there came a voice,
        like the growling of thunder;
        but as soft as butterfly sneezes,

Please, STOP.

The voice seemed to come from
   the mountain who rumbled,
   "Sometimes I see God
   swimming, in the dark blue
   depths of the sea."

And from the ocean who sighed,
   "He is often among the
   snow-capped peaks,
   reflecting the sun."

From the stone who said,
   "I sometimes feel her breath,
   as she blows by."

And from the breeze
   who whispered, "I feel
   his still presence as I
   dance among the rocks."

And the star declared,
   "God is very close;"
   and the island added,
   "His love touches everything."

And after a long,
lonesome and scary time . . .

. . . the people listened,
    and began to hear . . .

And to see God in one another . . .

. . . and in the beauty of all the Earth.

And Old Turtle smiled.

And so did God.